Mr. Putter & Tabby
See the Stars

CYNTHIA RYLANT

Mr. Putter & Tabby
See the Stars

Illustrated by
ARTHUR HOWARD

sandpiper

Houghton Mifflin Harcourt
Boston   New York

To Rebecca Howard and Sophia Howard
—A. H.

Text copyright © 2007 by Cynthia Rylant
Illustrations copyright © 2007 by Arthur Howard

www.hmhco.com

First Harcourt paperback edition 2008

Library of Congress Cataloging-in-Publication Data
Rylant, Cynthia.
Mr. Putter & Tabby see the stars/Cynthia Rylant;
illustrated by Arthur Howard.
p.   cm.
Summary: When Mr. Putter cannot sleep after eating too many
of Mrs. Teaberry's pineapple jelly rolls, he and Tabby take a
moonlit stroll that ends with the perfect neighborly gathering.
[1. Cats—Fiction.   2. Neighborliness—Fiction.
3. Night—Fiction.]   I. Howard, Arthur, ill.   II. Title.
III. Title: Mr. Putter and Tabby see the stars.
PZ7.R982Mub   2007
[E]—dc22   2006024326
ISBN 978-0-15-206075-6
ISBN 978-0-15-206366-5 (pb)

Manufactured in China
SCP 21 20 19 18 17 16 15
4500811987

1
Logs

Mr. Putter and his fine cat, Tabby,
loved to sleep.
They could sleep anywhere.

They slept in chairs,

in swings, in cars,

in tubs, and sometimes
in the laundry room.

Mr. Putter and Tabby also slept in a bed.
Of course, most of the time, sleeping in
a bed was just fine.

Mr. Putter plumped his pillow.
Tabby squished hers.
And then they slept like logs.

But one night, one of the logs
could not sleep.

2

Grumble

Mr. Putter was the log
who could not sleep.
He could not sleep
because he had eaten too many
pineapple jelly rolls
at Mrs. Teaberry's house.

Mrs. Teaberry was Mr. Putter's
good friend and neighbor,
and she liked to feed him.
She liked to feed everybody.
But most of all, she liked to feed Mr. Putter.

She was always sending her good dog, Zeke,
over to Mr. Putter's house with a note.
The note always said, "Are you hungry?"
And Mr. Putter always said, "Yes."
So he and Tabby went next door a lot.

But tonight Mr. Putter had been having
such a good time that he lost track and ate
twenty-one jelly rolls.

He forgot to count them as he popped them
one at a time into his mouth.

Before he knew it, twenty-one
jelly rolls were gone, and it was time
to go home.

Mrs. Teaberry was happy that Mr. Putter enjoyed her jelly rolls so much.
But Mr. Putter's stomach was not.
It grumbled and grumbled and grumbled.

Mr. Putter looked at his nice soft bed
when he got home.
G-R-U-M-B-L-E grumbled his stomach.
Mr. Putter knew he would not
be able to sleep
with all that grumbling.
What to do?
Mr. Putter looked at Tabby.
Then he got an idea.

3

Stars

"Let's go for a walk," Mr. Putter said.
He put his coat back on.
He put his hat back on.

He picked up Tabby.
And out the door they went.

It was a beautiful night.

The moon was full, and moonlight
was everywhere.

Tabby looked. She listened.
She twitched her ears.
She twitched her tail.
She loved the night.
Mr. Putter loved it, too,
even with a grumbling stomach.

Mr. Putter looked up at the sky.
He showed Tabby the stars,
and he told her all about them.
He told her that the Big Dipper
was full of milk
from the Milky Way.
Tabby purred. She loved milk.

He told her about looking at stars
when he was a boy.
And how he had always wanted to ride
in a rocket ship.
He told her how he had always
dreamed of adventure.

Tabby purred some more.

Mr. Putter and Tabby made a nice big circle around the neighborhood.

They looked at the sky.

They looked at the yellow lights of the houses.

They looked at cats sitting in windows,
looking back at them.

And when at last they circled back home,
they stopped in front of Mrs. Teaberry's house.
Mrs. Teaberry and Zeke were on the front lawn!
"Mrs. Teaberry, what are you doing up?"
asked Mr. Putter.

"Zeke has a grumbling stomach,"
said Mrs. Teaberry.
"He ate too many jelly rolls and we can't sleep."

Mr. Putter and Tabby were delighted.

They sat on the lawn with

Mrs. Teaberry and Zeke.

Mr. Putter's stomach and Zeke's stomach
talked to each other while
Mr. Putter and Mrs. Teaberry
talked to each other.

They told stories in the moonlight.

They told secrets.

They made each other laugh.

Then when the stomachs on the
front lawn stopped grumbling,
everyone said good night,
went to bed, and slept like logs.

In the morning, Mr. Putter heard
a scratching at the door.
He opened it.

It was Zeke with a note.

The note said, "Are you hungry?"

Mr. Putter smiled.
He picked up Tabby and
together they walked next door.

The illustrations in this book were done in pencil,
watercolor, and gouache on 250-gram cotton rag paper.
The display type was set in Minya Nouvelle, Agenda, and Artcraft.
The text type was set in Berkeley Old Style.
Color separations by SC Graphic Technology Pte Ltd, Singapore
Production supervision by Christine Witnik

Series cover design by Kristine Brogno and Michele Wetherbee
Cover design by Brad Barrett
Designed by Arthur Howard and Brad Barrett